Love Heist Pursuit

Shevnonvia Scott

Published by Shevnonvia Scott, 2022.

LOVE HEIST PURSUIT

First edition. November 20, 2022.

Copyright © 2022 Shevnonvia Scott.

ISBN: 979-8218114169

Written by Shevnonvia Scott.

*To all my **Family** and **Friends,** I just want to say thank you for all your support and believing in me, and to my **Mother,** she is my **Rock** and **Foundation**. I just want to let her know, that without her, I would have not made it this far. So thank you mom and to my Friends, I hope you love this book as much as I enjoyed making it, and to my soon-to-be **Fans,** who have yet to read this amazing book. It's a book I made to give you adventure and love, so please read it and share it with the people that you love.*

Love ✛ Heist ✛ Pursuit

Chapter 1
Stakeout

In the early morning around 3:45 a.m., a black Sudan showed up in front of an apartment. While detective Seth ross was in another Vehicle across the street in a dark navy blue tented window truck, along with his partner Daniel Higgens looking from afar for a drug dealer in a drug heist. Seth turns to his partner laughing saying, "Higgens our party is about to get ratchet, I can feel it, a tingling sensation in my toes man"

Daniel distinctively jogged his memory, "that's what you said last time," Seth quickly responds back "well, last time I thought I had the right guy, give me a break geez!"

Daniel taps him on his shoulders, telling him to hush, " look he's coming out, and he has a woman in handcuffs, she could be a hostage, but wait until they pull off to dim your lights, and follow them."

Dimming down his light as he pulls out on the main highway. At least 800 feet behind them, the two detectives, reposition themselves on another road, so they can be on the lookout once more.

Seth tries to convince Daniel "we might have a better view if we get out checking the woods." Daniel replies, "No way! we're staying put, last time, I caught a stray bullet because of you." Seth keeps reinsuring him, "it will be different this time, come on!" Daniel still refuses until multiple, shots went off in the distance. Both men looked at each other, and Seth gave him a shrugged eye, Daniel with a flustrated face tells him " Huaa, okay." Seth cranked up his truck to start getting back towards their location. Daniel dials for their unit to come on pursuit, Seth stops on the corner edge, 10 feet from the path opening, both getting out to grab their bulletproof vest, and weapons, heading down a woodland area.

Seth and Danial got down hearing bullets fly. Ducking, moving at the same time behind bushes waiting until their unit arrives, Daniel speaks on his vest walkie-talkie asking how close they were,? the Unit responded ("we are 15 minutes from your location lieutenant, just hang tight, help is on its way.") Seth shakes his head " their not going to make it in time Daniel, it's now, or never. We could lose this opportunity." Daniel is in panic mode, witnessing what his partner is about to do, shouting! "no, no, God dame it." Seth takes off in a rush, to a nearby bush trying to get closer, to see if he spots their suspect. Daniel comes up right behind him responding. "As soon as we get a break in the crossfire proceed". Seth yells! " I see him with an opening," both men started shooting the gunmen, trying to separate the dealer inside a shootout, finally, their unit arrives on scene.

WITH A FULL-BLOWN ATTACK, creating coverage, Daniel in excitement yelled, " yeah! my man, our cavalry is here. "That means I don't have to get shot this time because of you!" Seth grins reloading his gun. He runs to catch up with the suspect, restraining him to the ground, he calls out his name reading him his rights. "Jack Cleesit, you are under arrest, turn face down on your stomach with both arms *above you, and with your legs straight behind, he hurries to kneel cuffing him.*

Jake clashes with Seth, "you're making a huge mistake man. You just don't know it yet." Seth tells him "we'll see about that, now show me where you're holding the girl?" Jack disputedly replies " Yo! what girl? Seth yells to him" the girl we've seen tagging along with you in handcuffs", look don't play dumb amnesia games with me okay, where is she?." Daniel walks up whispering in his ear to inform him, "she ran off during the shot out". Seth angrily responded, "don't worry, she can't hide forever". He began shoving him inside his petrol truck. Next following day, Seth woke up on his day off, receiving a phone notification from Creinna Barcan. A female he met on a dating site, they were conversating for about a month now. Until she sent a text message, finally wanting to meet with him and Seth agreed.

He stood waiting patiently next to an Italian restaurant called Boenolee's in the Seattle bay area. Seth tries tediously, to lick his hands, in order to smooth out a loose strand of hair sticking up, nearby one of the restaurant windows. Using boastful encouraging words to himself saying, "you're an irresistible homicide detective, who is about to land an amazing hot chic today." Ow! too steamy to quit," and just then without him realizing it, she pin-pointed him standing there talking to himself, he jumped noticing her reflection showing up in the window.

Creinna responded "who's too steamy to quit? I thought I was the only woman, you're taking on a date today." Seth turns to her laughing, in embarrassment. "Oh no, I was just talking to myself, wait that came out wrong, hum! what I meant to say was. Is no object, or profile on a computer, nor, a window can do you, justice, in a reflection of my eyes." He puts out his hand, for her to take. Creinna smiled in amazement at his swift comeback.

THE TWO SHARED AN ELABORATE early dinner together, laughing having a good conversation, and winding up spending the whole entire day enjoying each other's company. Afterward, Seth takes her for ice cream, strolling down a sidewalk strip. Creinna said to him, "okay, so we already narrowed down my bio so far with my parents, where I lived recently before Seattle and my past deadbeat ex-boyfriend, and where I am working which I told you about, as a professionalized repair jeweler, and an experienced computer technician. Hum! let's see, what else am I forgetting ?" Seth utters to her saying I don't know you tell me, Creinna then said "Nope! I think that covers it," Seth twisted his nose cutely asking "your sure?" laughing with her, while she licks her ice cream remarking, "well is everything about what you've shared summed up." Seth squints his left eye saying, "yeah, I'm as good as I'm going to get."

He swiftly grabs her close, staring into her hazel grayed eyes to compliment her, "you're a sparkling rare gemstone, taking me on a remarkable journey, I could never think possible." He moves in close for a kiss but before he does, she wipes an ice cream mustache off of his upper lip. "Oh no!, I still have ice cream on me, I'm sorry," with a quick turn, he picks up his bottom right-sleeve shirt, whipping off his lips. Then looked up, laughing with her saying, "now let's try this again." She immediately agrees, the kiss sends static blows throughout his entire body, overshadowing gleaming street lights, and sounds from city traffic became silent, as the whole world around them moved at a steady pace. While blurs of a shallow background image circled. In a turning sequence, he knew after all that time of waiting, having side chicks, and one-night stands or platonic relationships never amounted up to this. She became a contender, I mean number one contender. Both stopped for a brief moment, and to his surprise, she realized the same scenario too, in a tight-hold grin kissing on again.

Storming in late, Seth brought everyone coffee along with turkey croissant breakfast sandwiches. Knocking on Daniels's office door smiling and telling him " we need to talk fast!" Seth hands him his coffee with a croissant asking him. "When did you know, Tiffany was the one?" Daniel stared confused in his office chair, answering him back. "Why do you ask ?" Seth runs his hands through his hair in disbelief saying "because I think I've found my soul mate man!," Daniel in excitement gets up from his chair and close's his office door from prying eyes, running back to his seat, Seth told him everything about his day off with Creinna yesterday.

DANIEL CHUCKLES "SEE what I told you, bro! about getting back out there dating." You were so obsessed over Lena for too long, for 3 whole years, 3 whole miserable years. Wasting all your time and efforts over a monstrosity. Told you her Gold-digging ass wasn't worth it, developing wrinkles above your eyebrows, and forehead, and for what? Lena!." Seth tries to calm him down agreeing with him, in aggravation. "Okay, you were right, I missed out on how it could be dating, and meeting new people but let's not forget. I was exploring different women occasionally, so I am not completely out of touch." Daniel shakes his head in disagreement "yeah, but not on real dates, that make you see things when you kiss them and shit. Not like those kinds of dates, you just admitted it. Hell! you just said it," (Seth fans his right hand twice drinking coffee in the other.) "Alright you caught me, yeah that's what I said." They both looked at each other, and picked up their coffee cups, to clink them together. Seth threw back in Daniel's face reminding him," don't forget I was the one who set you up with Tiffany."

DANIEL WITH A STRONG come back " True, true but I was the one who told you to get back out there and to set up your dating profile, so my good deeds are paid in full." Seth counters back. " No! not until you become my best man like I was attending your wedding. Only then will your contract be fulfilled, my friend." Daniel laughs and says "alright, alright." But just in between their conversation, Secretary Ellen Harper just informed them Chief Thomas, and agent Holden would like to see them, in his office A.S.A.P., Both men rushed to his office.

Chapter 2
Undercover Heist

Upon entering Daniel and Seth recognized the same guy they were tailing for two weeks straight, sitting comfortably there without handcuffs on. Daniel asked in a dumbfounded amusing manner.

" Hey, Chief what is he doing, sitting down in your office without any shackles on?". Chief Thomas glared in a furious mood. "Sit down gentlemen both of ya!" Seth hesitates to sit at first asking "what's going on?" looking at the guy while he stares back at them shaking his head and grinning.

Chief Thomas answers, "Don't you two remember government officials, sent over a professional theft agent, from the Internal affairs association? I told you he was going to assist with our heist case. I needed you two to study those documents, which I left pacifically on both of your desks. Well! did you see it, sitting there?" both men lied saying, " Yes Chief, of course, we did."

Chief Thomas felt disappointed, "we'll revisit this subject later, but for now, I wanted to introduce agent Christopher Holden. The three of you are going to get much acquainted, working together until you catch Conner Holden, his brother who works for one of the latest drug lords in town. Which happens to be their very own mother, Carmon Holden."

SETH GAZED OVER AT Christopher unsettled. "Wow! it's like a whole family affair Involvement."

CHIEF THOMAS INTERVENED, "shut up! At least he's not the two lazy idiots. Who forgot to read their profiles, but we don't have time for this argument, now do we? Carmon is on the move, for the next major drug heist. While his brother Conner was calling trying to act like someone else to check on Christopher here.

See to his knowledge, he thinks we don't know what he looks like, by him putting on different disguises, and masking his tone of voice but we have surveillance footage along with a voice analysis system. So, we know it's truly him."

Daniel reciprocated, "but if you know it's him why not pick him up from that exact location and book 'em? Plus make him confess, about everyone else involved instead of doing all of this?"

Chief Thomas reacted "Of course, we could do that. But this is when it gets more trickier and complicated. If we pursue them now, there is no guarantee we are going to catch his mother or bring in the stolen jewelry. Even a major key player called Davien Besten, he's been on our hit list for quite some years now. FBI, Secret service, and the whole military division wants him bagged. Heck! I even want him, just talking about him." (Chief Thomas grabs walnuts. From the edge of his table while taking a sip of peach soda.)

"Just knowing he could be in close proximity. Including his mother and his brother, that's like winning the lottery 30 times over. Our department precinct could be rewarded, for a big heist tip such as this. Shucks! I might receive a reward too from this situation, retirement even, set with full benefits and free medicare. Seth quickly adds"can we be honored too?, that would look exceptional on my resume Sr.,"

Daniel looks at Seth and laughs, commenting "yeah we do need a promotion, Tiffany and I wanted to buy a brand new house, you know it's getting overly crowed with the four kids and all."

Christopher blows a gasket over Chief Thomas along with the two men's disrespect. " Hey I am still in the room, don't forget the CIA made it pretty clear if I helped you catch my family members, years are deducted from their jail sentences. So, I don't appreciate you three goats, sitting here while my family is being the butt end of your stupid fucked-up jokes. It's pretty simple you help me save my family members, and I help you catch and bring them in, the discussion ended". Chief Thomas sincerely apologizes to Christopher. Asking him politely, to go sit in their waiting room. Christopher walks out giving all three men a provoked expression.

SETH CONTINUES IN AN awkward sarcastic manner, "So is it okay to go now ?" Chief reminds them both, "for now on read your assignments because if I catch, or even hear you've brought the wrong person in again. You won't have to worry about promotions, you will be demoted. Which means, I will get rid of you, having you both unemployed in a burger joint flipping burgers. I don't believe this would make Tiffany, or your kids very happy, stuck in that small suburban tiny home now would it?." Daniel answers in a slow saddened voice " no Sr." Chief Thomas turns his eyes to Seth, Let's not forget your whole family served under me as cops. You don't want them catching word, you've gotten too lazy to read, that's embarrassment beyond embarrassment. It makes people wonder, how you passed your academy exam, to get in here. Now leave me, both of ya!, so I can finish eating my walnuts in peace." They started to leave when Seth makes a stupid comment before walking out. "Chief, you just said, to leave you alone to finish your Nuts! get it? (wal-nuts)." Both men laughed out

loud, as the Chief mocked them laughing, and throwing a hand full of nuts in their faces, shouting " Get out, and stay out!"

Daniel stopped by Ellen Harper's Desk, telling her to page Christopher, to the conference room to discuss their mission.

Christopher enters making fun of the two men, while walking in, with a smirk on his face getting them back from earlier. "Well isn't it dumb and dumber, wanna-be detectives arresting the wrong man? Come on ladies and gents, let's hear it, a round of applause, for the Chief's two crack butts. He clapped together his hands, setting down, and crossing his arms.

Daniel forwards his comments, "technically to us you are still a bad guy, cause why would the Internal affairs want to capture your whole family, using you as bait? So, as far as I'm concerned, you deserve those cuffs the other night." Seth instantly agreed with him saying "that's right, what he said."

Christopher responded back " all I know is if you both strew this up, yall homies, won't have badges to hide behind. Especially if my family dies over yall bull-shit."

SETH ASSURES HIM, " well luckily for us. You don't have to worry your sweet little head about it."

Daniel nods in agreeance with Seth " Yep, dog, !" were non-Disposable.

Christopher begins to feel annoyed, wondering how he got set up with two lunatics. He speaks in avoidance talking under his breath. " What was the CIA thinking? hatching me up with these two morons is beyond me. If my family dies, I'm sending them straight to the dame morgue."

Daniel just looked at him wanting to fight, from his bold-full words."Excuse me, what did you say about us?." Seth held Daniel's shoulders and said: " Hey come on man, he's not worth flexing your muscles for right now, save your energy for the real mission okay." Daniel calm himself, as they both sat down.

Seth tries to talk to Christopher with a settled voice. " Hey, look we aren't here to fight you, man!

But only here to help. We want to know why you think your family needs to be saved despite the situation their in now?."

Christopher speaks in an angry tone. "Man forget yall, now you suddenly care about me, when the two of you, cut jokes in your Chief's office. Planning futures off of my family's expense. I'm out of here bro, thanks, but no thanks!

Chief Thomas hears the commotion, taking place from down the hall. He rushes over to see what was going on, then stares at the two men and said. "What did you, buffoons do now?"

Daniel spoke innocently " nothing Chief he's overreacting, like a clown."

Christopher shows an awkward face, repeating; "I'm overreacting these two fools aren't trying to help me, especially Dawn Wan! *over here."*

Daniel claps back, "Hey homie! get your name-calling facts straight it's Daniel okay!"

Christopher replied " yeah whatever, "Retarded semi-twins,"

Chief rapidly tells them all to shut up, and reminded Christopher " you don't have a choice here, but to comply with us, or it's back to the CIA slammer you go. And I can tell them, you were non-compliant, along with the years you wanted to knock off, for your family disappears drastically. So get in there, cooperate and do what, you've promised". The Chief walks back to his office. Christopher goes back inside the conference room sitting down.

Seth felt regretful "hey look we're sorry, let's start over okay. Could you start by filling us in a little about your father Alexander Holden". Christopher begins to answer their questions.

"YOU WERE RIGHT, HELPING the CIA catch my mom and my brother for less time, isn't the whole Ordeal. " When my mother was 25 years old, she took over the family business, leftover in my father's will. Other crime lords never really took her seriously, because she was a female, but my dad's trusted bodyguards always had our backs so we never had to worry about that. See for years my mother wanted to know what happen to my father and how he died. We were told, someone killed him. But we never knew who for sure. Till one day arriving from school early, I found her arguing with one of my dad's best friends, in our living room, his name is Davien Besten." (Christoper studders for a few seconds staring coldly down at the table holding back tears, trying to speak.)

Seth quickly offers him a piece of paper towel as tears stream down his face. He struggles but speaks again. "I overheard it, straight from her mouth like it was yesterday. She yelled to him pushing him away saying "my husband's death wasn't part of your deal." Davien cruelly lashed back. while I hid in the other room closet, crying couldn't believe my ears. She was also sleeping with this dude too, learning my youngest sister isn't my whole-blooded kin bro! she's my half-sister. Davien was one of my father's best-of friends, I thought to myself mom why? I was only 17 years old when this happened."

Daniel feels remorse. " Sorry about earlier, I know this is a lot to rekindle again. Since you've told this story already to the Fed's, and to our Captain. But we would like to know how Davien killed him?" Christopher continues " Davien was always jealous of my father. Business, wife, kids, money, and estate you name it. It was as if, he wanted to become an exact replicant clone of my father. So, he misled my father and mother about this big trade taking place under a local bridge in laguna beach California. He told my dad how much money to bring diamonds and all, so he trusted Davien's info only to be double-crossed, and executed by the Triad."

"Davien lied cowardly, telling us it was an ambush when really it was a betrayal. So, once she found out what he did, they were arguing back and forth, and she told him to leave. But he refused, confessing his love, by saying he did it so they could be together. That's when I walked in as he was leaving. She tried to console me saying she was sorry but, I wasn't hearing it man..! From then on, we never told my siblings all what really happened, I tried to help her with selling merchandise to keep our family business afloat. But I mistakenly got caught in Bermuda, making a couple of trades. My brother and mother tried to hire a lawyer to overturn the verdict against me. But since then I was serving prison time, as he reluctantly carried on with business procedures for 2 years. That's until Agent Prickem my handler, came to me and offered a plea deal to save my family for fewer years and I accepted."

Daniel asked more questions to Christopher. " There's one more question I wanted to ask, what exactly are you afraid your mom might do, for wanting to save her?"

Christopher responds, "plain and simple she's on the war path right now. You know the saying ain't nothing like a woman's scorn. Know this, my mother may have cheated on my dad, but she still loved my father. Davien to her was just a side thing going, she swore to me nothing more nothing less. She changed drastically over his death, eliminating anybody like a straight-up dude, all while wearing an innocent face. So, she vowed to me and, my siblings, she will take Davien down by any means necessary destroying his operations, hiring an insider personnel, using them to find out his trade dealings, and delivering poison to all of his clients.

Seth finally gets the plan, finishing Christoper's sentence. "So, when his shipment arrives, to his client's. That's when your mother's informant figures out or, finds the exact drop-site location and poisons *the products. Leaving Davien's clients to immediately think he went* <u>Rogue </u>*on their whole program. Killing him, using the same Triad members, who outs your father all those years ago, coming full circle."*

Christopher nods replying. " You got it sherlock! Using his own crew-mates to crucify his narrow ass."

Daniel was still confused, "okay but why go through all this trouble, why not kill him herself, once her intel personnel tracks his secret hideout." Christopher tells him "Davien doesn't always assist his men in a trade or heist, it would have to be dealing with a lot of money, and bigger clients in order to have him in the same place at the same time, plus he is more advanced. We're talking big leagues, over the continent-type stuff, he has houses everywhere. He even goes by multiple aliases, making it difficult for the Feds and his enemies to pinpoint him."

Seth comments, looking at Daniel worried. "So in other words we're dealing with one of those Pthanm ghosted criminals".

" Christopher grins saying no he is a ghost. That's exactly what I've been trying to tell everybody. The only way my mom and, I could get close to him, is by hiring low-ended drug dealers to ask if it was any hard drops happening. Even then, those leads were running cold. So, we had to think logically, in order to hire someone more high-end this time instead of low-end, someone who didn't have anything to do with our situation at all, and who can infiltrate some of his small jewelry heists, or drug bust before any of us could. So we needed to recruit someone smart and intelligent with computers. My brother did some digging, and found a tech nerd thief, from college, who works as an undercover computer technician, and owns her own company, dressing like a modern-day Burce Wayne in the streets, and by nightfall, becoming a Cat woman stealing shit, or should I say. Stealing from Upper-classed rich folks, and giving it to the poor." Daniel and Seth looked at each other, on Christopher's misinterpretation of theatrical

movie characters. Seth replies, "I think you mean richer and give it to the poor, right?"

Christopher nods his head saying "that's what I said Bro!."

Daniel rolled his eyes, glancing a little at Seth " No, not really but hum! don't worry man we will work together to save your family." Just remember to leave us the name of your informant, your family hired on our secretaries desk alright."

Once Seth arrived home, he jumps straight into the shower. Afterward, he texted Creinna "hey are you busy because, I was thinking of you, all day." Listen, one simple phone call, just won't do. I want to see you tonight maybe catch a bite to eat or, snuggle up or something". Creinna messaged him back, "I'm really back up at work right now, can I get a rain check". He texted back to her comment. "well I was looking forward to seeing you but if a rain check is what you need then okay. In the meantime, my heart will grow a little fonder of you. So, just let me know what day". She replies "I promise I will let you know." She takes off her face mask, after already coming from a jewel heist for a client. Looking at her phone smiling excited to see Seth again.

DANIEL CALLS SETH THE following morning. Filling him in on Christopher's informant's name, "her name is Rachel Bennett, and she has her own computer technician business." She is 34 years old and loves buying expensive things like couture clothing on a regular, Jewelry, yachts, dining in gourmet five-star restaurants, and buying, or renting out castle-like sculptured houses in multiple exotic places, and European cars fit for royal taste buds. Her net worth overall, including extra-curricular activities, which means posing as a vigilante Cat burglar. Bringing it to a grand total of 6.4 million dollars. Seth gives a hard low whistle inside the coffee shop," Dame! she doesn't even have to work. Tell me why this girl is still working?." Daniel laughs, to himself, "that's what I was saying, Bro! Is it because she's greedy or bored?"

Seth finishes his train of thought "No causes, homegirl, she's a bonafide hustler." I mean you just said it from the beginning that she likes expensive things. Do you have a visual of what she looks like?"

"No, were not allowed to access her full facial identity just yet, because Chief said the CIA only wanted her alias to remain strictly a secret for now. They don't want to give her position away and mistakenly blow her cover. Because in some ways Christopher struck a deal with her as well, to wipe her slate clean, of any crimes that were committed. In her name since this whole fiasco started, in order to keep all of her business-related assets in tacked."

"So, in a way she's like a double agent, working for us because of Christopher and his mom all at the same time. But I seriously doubt, the CIA will keep its promise, for a full slate agreement. Rachel and Christopher will still have to do some time after all this is over."

Seth agrees with him, sipping on his cappuccino, turning around and bumping into Creinna by accident, almost spilling his drink on her blouse. He quickly tells Daniel "hey I'll see you in 20 minutes", and immediately hangs up, speaking in a startled tone. "Hi, I see we have something else in common."

Creinna said, "like what exactly?"

Seth answered her smiling holding up his cup of cappuccino. " Coffee shops," she said her apologies for taking a rain check last night. He then tells her, "well my beauty is here now that's all that matters, and I am a savaged beast just waiting to be tame into an honest man". She laughs at his swagger come back. She replies impressed, "Tosha! " so how long have you been practicing that corny line Lieutenant Fabio? Before bumping into me."

"It just magically appeared," Seth picked up her right hand which was free, as she holds her coffee in the other, " see you bring stuff like that out of me, you know, I blame you". Then she rolled her eyes and giggled, "I'm not building you up to say all those things, no sir. You came up with all those, on your own."

He shakes his head saying, "you know exactly what voodoo spell rituals you be brewing, with those grayed hypnotic hazel eyes. Having me all twisted, and weak in the knees hearing theme music and shit. A brother can't function on a daily basis. Steady contemplating when our next encounter is taking place. Please, say you can make time for me tonight, if not I'll skip work for you right now, and I suggest you do the same."

Creinna looked him up and down like he was losing his mind. "You're crazy! I can't do that my bosses will literally kill me or, I can even lose my job."

An idea dawned on Seth. "Okay, I guess I can wait until Friday night he mumbled". Creinna could barely hear him mumbling to himself.

"You said what? I can't understand that Mumbo jumbo."

"I said, well perhaps, I can wait until this weekend or Friday whichever you prefer."

Creinna gets close like she was going to give him a goodbye kiss. He intently holds his breath, a little just slightly taking her all in. From her perfume down to her lips, and the way she talked softly. She then moves toward his left cheek with her neck bent to the side, saying; "Friday, it's a date," as she turns and walks away, waving saying "see you this weekend." He almost drops his cappuccino yet again. While his mind was still swirling in a deep daydream thought once more. Watching her body move to only him, it seemed as if time has frozen, just like that night on their first date. As she fades out of view, time with everyone around him switched back to normal. People were moving at their original speed again, but his love song still plays on in his head, even after she leaves.

Arriving at the precinct, and hearing his private epic love song beating on as a techno series. He finally reached his desk flopping hard in his chair, holding both hands on his chin and, looking at a blinking cursor on his computer screen. A faint noise of some sort, called his name from a distance, hitting his desk with a stack of papers on the right side of him. He then snaps out of his daydream sequence with the music coming to a stretching halt. He gradually looked up and saw Daniel calling him from his office desk.

Daniel looked at him saying " what the fuck man, what were you doing? you said 20 minutes, hell 20 minutes turned into 45 minutes. I kept looking at my watch, and saying dang where is this fool? Now your straddling up in here, like you don't have a clue or something. Earlier you sounded different and ready to work on the phone; now you seem sluggish as if you hadn't gotten a good night's sleep. What's wrong with you? You ain't pissing the bed at night, is it? because if you are, you know your my friend, right?. I will go to a local convenience store for you right now and purchase you some of those grown men panty underwear's called Depends. You know the kind that looks like boxers, not the diaper ones."

Seth straightens up his face in an awkward look towards his friend responding " NO you don't have to do that please don't. It's Creinna I saw her again man. I never felt this way about any female before bro! I mean anybody not even Lena."

DANIEL SPEAKS WITH a light bulb, dawning on him finally. "Oh, so you are out of sorts because of her? Man, I thought how the way you were walking in slow motion in here. I thought you might have gone to the back room where they hold all the evidence and drugs."

Seth gave Daniel an insane look and responded " Hey, yo what? what are you talking about man?"

Daniel began to fill him in on why Eric, big busty Charlene, and Brandon, go to the back evidence room sometimes. Seth still seems dumbfounded about what he's talking about. Daniel continued to tell him "it's because they're smoking the evidence man, yeah! I found out from Joe this morning. Every day around this same exact time, they do the whole head turning side to side from their seats. To make sure no one is watching, and slowly moves down the hall, making it inside the evidence room." Seth drops his mouth in disbelief, closing the door of Daniel's office. Rubbing his head to say, "it's starting to make so much sense now. With the stumbling coming from the back every other day, with their eyes all wide 'n and dilated, smelling with deep poured-on cologne." Daniel then recounter, "see now why I thought you been hitting the back bro!, poof, poof, goes the Weasel."

Seth gave him, a come-on face. "Fool come on man, have more common sense, than that Daniel!"

Daniel continued joking, "Na, I mean Seth, I wouldn't have judged you, if you were doing it, or not. This job sometimes can be stressful".

Seth asked him sarcastically, " On a serious note, keep it 100. How many years you've known me, Daniel? "Well, whatever, water under the bridge man okay. Let's put the subject, back on Creinna shall we. Look every time I see her it's like this wired beating techno music sound. Coming through in my brain! with everyone freezing around me, in this daytime story episode."

Daniel explains the basic symptoms he had. "Okay with Tiffany it was nerves, mostly, palms sweaty, you know! the usual stuff people would relate to. Oh and like fireworks shooting when you're kissing them. But nothing like what you're describing."

Seth answers telling him, "Well, I guess maybe it's different for everyone because, I can feel the beat of the music, and it only happens when I see particularly just her. And memorizing her hazel eyes with her hour glassed bottled shaped body, and dark Sandie long hair and perfume smelling like citrus aqua rain with her, smooth looking semi-chocolate lips, skin just so, sooo ", Daniel waves his hands in front of his face saying, "congratulation dog! you are officially in my club now." Officer Benjamin Wakes opens the door and enters telling them "Christopher just heard back from his informant. They're having one of the jewelry trade drops tonight." Seth asked him "what about the drugs?" Officer Wakes reiterate, "no! nothing on drugs yet, Daniel then says okay "let's suit up!"

SETH GRINS " YOU KNOW who you sound like just now?" Daniel glanced over as they both suited up, walking to their unmarked truck hopping in. Seth re-enacts it, from a favorite sitcom TV show he watches all the time. "you sound like one of those superhero shows, I watch all the time like the Green Arrow." (Seth then tries to do a deep voice imitation of Oliver Queen. Mocking what Daniel said earlier "Let's suit up.") Daniel agrees to say "yeah man, of course, we're heroes. I mean if we don't acknowledge it for ourselves, no one else will." A call comes through their truck radio, while stuck in traffic downtown. Informing them to go to a warehouse on the outskirts near Chainer & Cole company, Seth picks up the communicator and responds "okay! thanks, we're heading there now. Hey, you might want to stop at a gas station to load up on food and gas."

Daniel agrees with Seth in a hurried voice. "We'll stop at one, on the way going". He found a small local gas station before heading to Chainer & Cole company 4 miles out. Meanwhile, Creinna is already on-site in her camouflage tent positioned east-west of the same location. She then gets her equipment ready, surveilling a digital format, map print of the Chainer & Cole warehouse company. She gets close to an easy entrance and an exit. Just in case things get hot and heavy she will know which escape route to take.

The two detectives finally made it to the Chainer & Cole company site, parking east in the back woodland area. Hiding their navy blue F-150 ford truck behind two big pine trees half a mile across the street. Seth picks up his binoculars to get a closer-range view of the warehouse. Daniel picks up his as well and tells Seth in a skeptical voice. " Davien has at least twenty men scouting the whole premises holding heavy artillery. Seth replies " hum! wouldn't you? His location gets hit up all the time, and while Harboring top-of-the-line jewelry with 100,000's lbs of drugs transporting in and out of state borderlines. I for one would have it barricaded and heavily guarded too, fenced with Pitbulls."

An 18-wheeler truck just showed up arriving at the gates, marked with the same name as the warehouse Chainer & Cole company. His armed men escorted out some of the workers, dressed in fumigated-masked, white coats unloading the truck. Both Daniel and Seth tried to adjust their binoculars to get a closer clear peek at the merchandise inside, but they were all boarded up in small wooden crates.

Daniel tells Seth " it will be better to wait until it gets a little darker around 6:30 p.m., close to 8:00 o'clock. That way, we can alert the unit to come in a decent matter of time. Seth agrees to say, "maybe reach out, 1 hour and a half prior because it takes at least 30 to35 minutes to get out here and set up properly." Daniel replies " yeah you're right 'cause it's 3:55 p.m. now. I'll call in the next two hours, Around 5:00 o'clock to give them some wiggle room."

Chapter 3
Heist Unravels

AS THE UNIT STARTS to arrive, to set up on the east side. Crienna , noticed a truck coming to pull up, she drags her tiny camouflage tent down into a deep sink under the rocks. Packing up her duffle bag storing guns and, grenades along with putting her throw quilt, over her tent with pine needle straws on top, to hide it.

She slowly moves down the ditch, crawling over rocky sloped rocks toward small bushes further east-south. As night falls, Crienna sees an opening to deploy her drone to drop a bomb, around the back entrance. She then puts on her night vision goggles. To have a visual of the loading dock, she tries to do it fast since the guards are circling the building every so often.

ONE OF THE UNIT'S FEMALE officers Radio in, to grab their attention of a small black object flying over the back building. Both Seth and Daniel picked up their binoculars and noticed it too. Seth squits his eyes and said, "what is that ?" finally one of the seal unit agents found out it was an explosive strapped to a drone. Officer Macy Tanner then calls back to notify all unit members "it's a bomb"!. As soon as Creinna had a targeted spot, she detonates the bomb. A huge explosion shook the foundation, dismantling the back wall. Suddenly Davien workers inside came out retreating from the engulfed flamed warehouse.

Macy Tanner informs everyone to quickly put on their night vision gargles to approach the warehouse.

Once inside the gates, heavy gunshots were firing. Both men ducked behind two work truck vehicles, as the rest of the unit stormed into a war shootout. Crienna then hurries carrying a cliffhanger-roped gun.

She climbs up the roof, keeping a low-ducked appearance during a black smoked mirage, as the men stayed stranded below, outside holding their own. She finds an opening to climb down, through an air conditioning vent. Having her night vision gargles on. Along with a smoke mask clutching her rope, sliding slowly down. Once inside, she immediately sees lots of men in white-coated suits running to put wooden crates inside a van, that wasn't damaged by the explosion. She runs across to a nearby office and uses their computer to quickly hook her USB notepad up, to download information, for Davien's next heisted locations.

BUT SHE NOTICED THE network was failing. She had to hurry, to finish before she loses any other data retrieved.

Luckily, she managed to collect all the information that was needed. Creinna disconnected from their computer database. While slipping her notepad into her small backpack, and trying to find another escape route. Since the route, she was originally going to take, was already mistakenly blown up, the unit poured inside. She then runs into an empty laboratory room, filled with different unknown chemicals, with an air conditioner ventilation system spotted on the ceiling.

WHEN ALL OF A SUDDEN, one of Davien's men came in holding his gun seeking refuge to hide. She ducks behind the steel cabinet and watches as he gets near to knock him out with an iron rod, laying next to her feet on the floor. Creinna moves fast to pick it up. As he starts to turn, catching a glimpse of her. She wacks him across his face, while he grabs pushing her, into the table filled with chemicals and choking her neck. She gazed to her right side and picks up a broken flask of glass, to luge in his throat. Blood protrudes out, as he collapses to the floor. Coughing from the struggle, she then climbs up through the air conditioning ventilation making it to the roof. Creinna climbs down, heading into the woods to locate her car. Meanwhile, 12 of Davien's men were captured while 8 managed to escape leaving some of the crates behind, and some workers were found dead, with only 11 remaining alive.

OFFICER TANNER STUDIED the surveillance footage before, and after the raid. To get a total headcount of workers who died out of the 37, verse those who are alive now.

She told them "it was at least 37 workers, and only 11 survived it, with Davien's men by itself, it was twenty like we predicted. Plus counting the men we caught verse, the ones who got away, apprehending a total of 12. Also, surveillance caught a black blur on top of the roof but couldn't make it out completely, or maybe it could have been just dark smoke from the explosion." Seth thanked officer Tanner for the info, and told the rest of their team, to gather what's left for evidence.

Later on that night Creinna arrived home to take a shower, only to find a tiny cut to her waist midsection. But it wasn't too bad, she was able to clean the wound and close it up. Soon after 30 minutes, Carmon called to check in.

CARMON ASKED IN AN *Anxious tone, "Rachel did you poison the diamonds," Creinna commented to say, "no it was too many of them, however, I did manage to gather data of locations for the next bust on a flash drive." Carmon responds "well done that's even better, you'll get him next time I'm sure of it. For now, get some rest we have a long grueling month ahead of us" (Carmon hangs up, and Creinna forwards the same message to Christopher). Seth then sends her a message as well saying "Friday is almost here, for me to take you out." She replies back, with a smiley emoji face, typing "can't wait."*

AROUND MID-MORNING, *a knock came on the door of Daniel's house with an old woman wearing a robe, and bedroom slippers. He realizes it was his neighbor from next door, Daniel told her "it's 4 am in the morning, Ms. Nancy, what's wrong?" Nancy responded worried saying. "I'm sorry, Daniel I know it's late, but coming down for a cup of coffee in my kitchen. There I saw, a weird shadow-looking man from my window creeping into your backyard. Just 15 minutes ago, running behind your shed carrying a brown paper bag of some sort."*

Daniel responds saying "Ms. Nancy I' 'll take a glance at my surveillance cameras okay, you shouldn't worry about these certain things, I got it." Just when he was about to close the door, her hands clutched on.

Nancy shrugs with an odd look, "Well I figured since you are part of the neighborhood watch committee you should know whoever this is, trolling around our community at night. Put some clothes on, and do some investigating". He rolled his eyes closing the door to retrieve his clothing.

His wife Tiffany woke up peeking her head, down the staircase asking, "who was that?" Daniel puts her mind at ease, "it was Ms. Naney at the door." Tiffany wondered why questioning her husband. " What did she want?" Daniel tells her, "she wanted me to check out something outside for her". Tiffany peered hard at him saying " it's 4 am in the morning babe! did she lose her cat, Marlo, again.?" Daniel commented back in exhaustion, "I don't know babe! go back to sleep."

TIFFANY RETURNS TO bed, while he puts on rain boots with his sweat bottom pants, and tank top, with a coat carrying a flashlight walking to the back yard. When he notices Ms. Nancy again whispering out of her screened curtain window. "Hurry before he gets away, you slow unfit monkey". He speaks back in agitation, "I'm going!" (while mumbling to himself), "I can't wait to get this dame drug heist over with. So, Tiffany and I can take the kids out of this hell hole, of nosey hypocrites." Just when he was approaching the shed he heard a clinking noise coming from the inside. He reaches for his gun shouting, to whoever was hiding in there. "Hey! this is the police come out with your hands up," he jumped back into a posed position with his gun, ready to fire. As the shed door flew open, Wilber the homeless guy. Held one hand up, with a licker bottle in the other. Shaking in fear "don't shoot Daniel it's me," Daniel then took a breath of relief, putting his gun back in his coat pocket. Asking him in a strange sentence. "'Wilber what are you doing here man? you scared the living crap out of me." 10-inch millimeter calibers were about to seep heavy colossal holes, tattooed to your ass just now."

Wilber answered, "I needed a temporary place to sleep, it was getting a little cold in the park all night when the temperature dropped."I'm sorry for waking ya!". Daniel then told him " come on, I have a pair of changeable clothes inside, you can take a shower in my guest bathroom. But throw that licker bottle inside the trash before you enter my house. You can also sleep in the guest bedroom okay, come on," Wilber thanked Daniel for his generosity.

DANIEL STILL FELT JET-lagged after last night's raid, and interruption of sleep because of his neighbor Ms. Nancy. Chief Thomas walks into his office telling him to come with me, also tapping on Seth's desk while he was on a phone call, by pointing towards his office, Seth quickly hangs up to follow. Chief Thomas closes his office door, in a Getty tone saying "We've found her, the woman who got away from Christopher the first time, during a drug bust, you two made 3 weeks ago, she arrived in a safe house earlier this morning. Agent Grant Prickem, Christopher's Handler picked her up on Pine street hiding in an abandoned constructed building last night around 11:30 p.m. just before midnight." Both men were in shock at her apprehension, Seth quickly asks "so what does she know?" Chief Thomas said, "she is the hitman or, should I say hit women paid to take out Mark Miller a Gardner of Davien Besten."

"Turns out he overheard some important information of Davien, leaked out about his involvement with city council women Georgia Fields. When he finished cleaning the pool, he then came inside to collect his payment from Davien. But, before he walked in, that's when he overheard about both of their plans to kill her running mate this election and orchestrate a streamlined profit lacing drugs and diamonds hidden in bags of sugar, dividing a chunk of dough amongst each other. Once he helps eliminate the competition for her, making it all seem like a freak car explosive accident gone wrong. Then Obviously leaving her automatically to be re-elected as mayor again. Allowing Davien to keep making trades in town. Mark made a mistake standing too close to the door, tripping on a loose piece of carpet. He managed to escape, sharing his story with the Feds. But of course, they thought it would be much safer to relocate him, and his family until this whole thing blows over. But there is some more juicy entertaining news. It seems the hitwoman squealed too. Giving up Davien's other client's location, begging to strike a deal for a release Pardon. So, now Agent Prickem with his team are now, on their way to pick them up, as we speak. This cuts Christopher and his family's sentence in half."

Daniel and Seth were surprised at how things are now progressing along so fast. Seth replies "man Chief I thought this kind of case would take forever to solve." Chief Thomas then shook his head in disbelief. "I know, I 'can't believe it either."

DANIEL SEES NOW WHY they wanted them to handle the case with Christopher and his informant. "It just occurred to me, the Feds just hired us, for an easy babysitting job while they're taking in all of the glory, capturing Davien Besten by themselves. Seth added, yeah bro! you're right, hey Chief does this mean we won't receive our raise? Daniel turns to Chief Thomas and tells him I can't spend another day

in that god-forsaken neighborhood, living in that tiny house Chief, I just can't. My neighbors are nosey and problematic."

Seth reminds Chief Thomas about the warehouse bust with crates filled with diamonds. "Yet I remind you, Chief, the other Officers and I risked our lives". Daniel calls out "don't forget the S.w.a.t team too, now if it wasn't for them we wouldn't have some of Davien's men setting in a jail cell right now." Chief Thomas Acknowledges their testimonies by adding, "your right, the CIA are getting too much glory credits these days, using us as pawns. To get ahead, on their mission endeavors, even though things seem bleak at times. I just want you two, to know how important all of you are in this department, and how much effort you put into what you do every day. So, that being said. I was way ahead of you."

He then pulls two letters of promotional checks out from his left desk drawer and rewards them, "you both deserve it."

Daniel rubs his checks, saying "thank you Sr., I've been looking forward to this for a long time." Chief Thomas smiles at the two of them. Seth adds, "I can take Creinna out to somewhere fancy now for our second date." They then shock his hand, walking out excitedly, and high-fiving the rest of the unit. With them showing off their checks too, Daniel makes a remark, "finally I can escape with my family to find a quiet neighborhood," both men laughing sitting in Daniel's office eating cold-cut sub sandwiches for lunch.

Meanwhile, at Seth's apartment, he gets comfortably situated calling up Creinna, she answers in a caring voice. "Hey stranger, what up?" Seth speaks back, "I'm setting on the couch relaxing, fantasizing about you right next to me, wearing nothing but purple satin lingerie, showing off your long sandy dark locks, crawling from the other end towards me. While I meet you halfway, gathering evidence from each angle of your body. (Creinna laughs softly as Seth continues talking.) once, you give me mutual consent, then I proceed to explore using my handcuffs, wrestling you up against my chiseled, muscled chest, as we make our way to my exotic cave, my animal instincts begin to kick in, and my X- rated vision scanners detect every inch of your curvy seductive figure."

Creinna listens eagerly on the other end while biting her lips visualizing his touch, as he explains his story step by step. But instantly got rudely interrupted by Carmon beeping through. Seth was still stuck in the moment talking about tracing his tongue from her belly button to taking off her underwear. She tells Seth to pause the fantasy talk for a moment, lost in his train of thought he mistakenly thinks she is calling his name out in ecstasy. Rolling her eyes in annoyance, she grabs for her alarm clock. Seth snaps out of his lusty imagination.

His voice grubbles, "Creinna why'd you stop me, we were just getting to the good stuff women !."

She says to Seth in remorse, "I'm so sorry, my boss is beeping in, I gotta take this call, but we will finish this tomorrow just text me the time, and place for our date okay."

He suggested a solution, "why don't I come to pick you up instead?" She laughs to say "you just want to know where I live, don't you?" Seth responds to himself out loud for her to hear, "Dame she guessed it." Creinna told him "okay, I'll text you my address". (Seth celebrates over the phone quietly) Telling her "okay hum! that's great, I'll pick you up at 8:00 p.m.," with her replying back to him "it's a date." They both hung up from each other, While Creinna calls Carmon back.

Carmon picks up, answering elated. "Rachel I have some thrilling news, my son crossed examined the file's you've provided, for Davien's next heist location, it was accurate, he called over to a hotel in Catalina Island in California. Portraying as a personnel security bouncer, checking on his reservation. Confirming his arrival tomorrow afternoon, early for his next trade on Saturday night. I will need you to make it over there early to inspect how many of his clients will attend, Davien's party summit. To see if the shipment of diamonds is stored nearby his hotel, releasing the poison. My son will accompany you on this journey". Creinna begins to ask, "what time to meet with him, and where?" She responded by saying "Conner plan's to leave on our private family helicopter at 7:30 p.m. late afternoon." Creinna replies hesitantly, "okay when does he expect us to be back in Seattle?" Carmon then wanted to know why. "Why! do you have other plans besides this?"

Crienna makes up a lie. "Yes! my father isn't doing so well, and I promised my mother I would stop by to have dinner with them around 8:00 p.m. in the afternoon."

Carmon is confused saying, "can't you do it a bit earlier Rachel? This mission is extremely important to me, and I don't know if it would wrap up in time." Creinna felt disgusted saying "sure okay." Carman responds, "Thank you, Rachel your hard work and loyalty haven't gone unnoticed. Now, remember my son will meet up with you at 7:30 p.m. tomorrow afternoon. Be sure to bring a few changeable clothes." Creinna then switches gears calling Seth back.

Seth picks up giving a romantic line, "I knew you couldn't sleep without, Robo sexy cop, putting you to bed." To his amazement, she agrees with him. Creinna tells Seth, "I'm skipping work tomorrow to be with you. How about I take a sick day and, I want you to do the same, we can meet up tomorrow morning around 8:00 a.m., what do you think?" He sets in silence, for a minute to catch his excitement, then answered "okay sounds good let's do it."

Seth calls into work, asking Daniel to cover for him. He tells Seth,"have a good time man! you deserve it, three years suffering from your crazy ex-girlfriend. Shows your long past, overdue for this." Seth responds "thanks homie", hanging up.

Chapter 4
Davien's Final stand

DRIVING WITH DIRECTIONS, Creinna gave to him. His Gps system leads the way toward a Ginormous penthouse, Seth glances over to his Gps, to make sure this was the right house, but every time he goes to check it, the system keeps reassuring him, he arrived at his destination. Getting out of his new white 2023 dodge charger, sporting a gray blazer to match Creinna's eyes, he began to approach to knock on her door, carrying a dozen of soft pink roses.

He hears her footsteps rushing to the door, Creinna yells, " I'm coming!" She opens the door dressed in a tight hugged long silk satin burgundy dress, with a laced flowered design trim along her side, showing off her bareback, with her hair curled in an upright position.

SPEECHLESS AS HE TRAILED his eyes from her head, down to her toes. Tongue-tied speaking slowly, "wow! Creinna no words can be found in the human vocabulary for what I'm thinking". Creinna laughs to say "are those for me?" Seth smiles nodding his head, handing over the pink rose bouquet. She invites him in, to take a look around,

"I'm going to put these in some water, come in and make yourself at home."

Exploring the view, of each hallway, and bedroom, he felt a little small as he looked up to the stairwell with a cathedral-like ceiling, and crowned molding fit for royalty, Seth was overwhelmed thinking to himself, as the marbled floors gleamed in clear reflection. He walked into one of the bathrooms gushing over how beautiful it all was. Creinna called his name, bringing him back to reality, asking him "are you ready to go, did you enjoy some of the tours?" Seth rubbed his chin replying "it's ___, what can I say it's huge". She smiles saying "well maybe when you are free one day. I can present you with the rest of the house okay. So where are you taking me on our second date adventure ?" He tells her, "it's a surprise."

SHOWING UP AT A RESTAURANT on the water, 20 minutes out of town approaching a large fiery boat ride, taking her hand, while the waiter asked for his reservations. Once they were clear aboard, he guided them toward their own private table. Near an ocean view, taking their brunch orders. As she whispered sweetly to him "you knocked it out of the park Robo sexy cop." (Seth grins, leaning over and tilting his shades) "you haven't seen, anything yet."

The fiery boat traveled across, taking them behind the mountain side to a water park community. Dropping them off, and scheduled to later return around 3:45 pm. Shopping center malls, bouquet stores, and restaurants stretched beyond the eyes can see. Seth smiles saying, "come on I'm taking you dancing, and afterward El Quads, it's a Mexican restaurant". Creinna's mouth expands in aw! He holds her hand guiding her to a club called Raw Spice. Immediately the bouncer lets them in by reservation Seth pulls her to the middle of the floor between a crowd, starting to dance. He grips Creinnas waistline as she wraps her arms around his neck. Both laughed as Seth twirls Creinna, and clutched her hips tight, moving seamlessly to a Jamaican R&B beat.

AFTER RAW SPICE THEY arrived in El Quads to eat, the whole evening wound down in a romantic merry-go-round, with Seth managing to get her back home at a decent time around 6:25 p.m., standing at her doorstep he gave her a kiss, telling her good night, as she said it back. Soon as he left, she quickly packed her duffle bags with changeable clothes to meet Conner at the docking airstrip around, 7:30 p.m. Conner peeked down at his custom Rolex saying "7:30 p.m. on the dot, let's board the helicopter". Creinna texted Christopher about Catalina Island, meanwhile in a bar cross-town, when a pining sound vibrated Christopher's phone, it was Rachel. He messaged her back and tries to warn the Feds as well.

CIA FEDERAL AGENT Grant Prickem received a message from Christopher shedding light on Catalina Island. Grant replied, telling him, "half of his team is already in Singapore arresting some of Davien's clients." So, Prickem texted his partner agent Felicia White to debrief the agency.

SETH BEGAN TO UNDRESS out of his gray suede suit at home, cutting on one of his favorite television shows. Fixing a glass of tequila, and avocado dip with nacho chips. Just when he was about to set down a knock came on the door of his apartment. It was Daniel with Agent Felicia White, alongside Christopher. Seth invites them in, Daniel gave him a cold stare " telling him "your cell phone is on silent, you might

want to switch it back on." Seth apologizes, when Felicia White updates his knowledge on everything. He answers wondering about a plan, "So what's next?" Agent White said to him "we need all hands on deck, to gear up, and tag along with me, and my squad. Chief Thomas figured you both might want in on the action since my comrade benched you. So, are you in, or out?"

Seth quickly spoke up," most definitely! I'm in". Both Daniel and Christopher chimed in "us too". Agent White said with a hyped-up voice, "Okay let's head out."

Reaching Catalina Island Creinna and Conner unboarded the helicopter retrieving their bags of artillery weapons. Worried Christopher with the CIA wouldn't make it there in time. She didn't want to poison anyone nor, end up on the wrong side to lose everything she worked so hard for. Mixing too deep with Carmon's family feud Vs. Davien Besten cost her a lot of headaches. Plus, Seth will never forgive her, once he finds out who she really is, and what she has done so far. They've chartered a luxury Bentley heading for the Fort Rouge hotel owned by Davien.

IN THE PRECINCT OF Seattle Felicia along with Chief Thomas, gathered all officers, and agents to deliver an encouraging speech.

"As I hold up this badge we instantly think of honor, truth, and justice. But for me, it's a symbol of a true human being who stands behind it, and for the men and women, we've lost. Behind enemy lines, this badge holds history, Privilege, and bloodshed. We ware their blood every day, for those who ware it for fame, glory, and attention will never have its full power of selflessness nor companionship towards our fellow man. Today I want to uphold your Oath, death comes to us all, but while we are alive and breathing, let our Perpetrators hear our wrath, know our guns, and clicks of our cuffs. Who's with me?"

The officers and agents cheered as Chief Thomas shakes Felicia's hands. She directed them, all aboard seven air crafts. Her agency supplied, heading towards Catalina Island. One rogue officer slips out of the crowd to warn Georgia Fields, who then relaid it to Davien Besten.

Chapter 5
Davien's capture

GEORGIA PANICS AS SHE tells officer Limmerman to move up their timetable on killing elective Iyana James. She signals a message to the other Triad members. Who are still undercover within the agency one state over in Oregon. To find out and locate Mark Miller's safe house in their system, and also the hitman Davien hired."No strings go unpunished. Oh! and Officer Limmerman sweetie! tell the Triad. Davien's checkerboard pieces have expired." Officer Limmerman answers back in amusement, "Okay my love." She calls Davien to give him a heads-up. Davien filled his clients in on unexpected visitors, locking, and loading for the company. Conner and Creinna made it inside the hotel dressed up to join Davien's party festivities, undercover at opposite ends of the room, he then stood next to a back exit steel door, while she is standing nearby the front entrance wall. knowing they would have to go through the kitchen cooler area to reach the diamonds. While Conner's other informant dressed up as a waiter, who arrived 1 day earlier, would have to confirm if the diamonds are indeed there. He awaits for him to respond through his earpiece, Creinna was hoping Christopher would have made it there, before now. But Davien came up dragging Conner's waiter informant out on stage in public

view making a speech, with Creinna in shock and Conner looking back at her saying "Rachel! abort, abort" in her earpiece. She tries to run, but two security guards approached her and another came from the back door.

DAVIEN PULLED OUT A long machete-daggered knife to slit Conner's informant's throat, proceeding to jab it through his upper chest cavity throwing him to the floor. And wiping it off on his suit with a handkerchief. (As both felt Disgusted) He makes an announcement to Creinna and Conner. "This is for my two guests. Didn't your mother ever tell you it's rude, to leave a party early? especially one, you weren't invited to. Maybe the after-party could be more entertaining." Creinna moves her left index finger to click on a distressed button located on her smartwatch signaling it to Christopher to track their location. She waits to activate the hydro sleep mode button until the two guards get them alone away from Davien's clients.

A DISTRESSED BEACON went off on Christopher's phone. He told Felicia, "my brother and Rachel are in danger, he found them out. Is it any tunnels we can take because 9 times out of 10 if he knows we're coming, Davien has spies everywhere?" Felicia makes a call and checks out her digital notepad to find the nearest route to settle down in California, she figures out a better plan from what they've discussed originally. "Let's divide our ranks, once we're on foot, we could diverge into four different groups. One will attack the tunnel ways, keeping some of our team air-born. Third unit who are excellent swimmers goes northwest bound. leaving the last group coming in on a southeast, front entrance." Seth listens to her alternative plan, saying "that's a pretty good idea". Felicia tells her pilot to set down in a nearby area to educate

their team. Davien's clients prepare for war, his men cover the front and back entrance. He tells his bouncer KC to lock them up inside the kitchen freezer. KC pushed Conner, and Creinna in the direction of their Freezer by gunpoint, with two other guards, accompanying him. As they were walking back towards the ballroom area, she gave Conner a hint. Creinna looked over at Conner yarning, "man! I'm tired," KC threatens her, " don't worry eternal rest awaits for you both inside our frosty freezer." All three security guards laughed, when Conner holds his breath, as she also breathes in, activating hydro sleep gas. By the time they reached the kitchen area, 5 minutes later, drowsiness started to settle in. Struggling to stay awake, one guard fell out. As Kc, and the other bouncer turns distracted. Quickly Creinna and Conner picked up heavy utensils to fight with. Blanking their eyes gathering the bouncer's guns, both helping each other out of the kitchen part, far from hydro sleep fumes.

Conner talks in a highly drunken state. "We can still pull this mission off Rachel." Creinna frowns with a printed senile look. " We almost died in there, are you insane? Live to battle another day, can't win something dead." Shadow step sounds of feet, were coming near. Underneath the dining ballroom door, she grabs Conner's arm around her shoulders, heading out the back door, but just then she sees two men looking in two opposite directions holding firearms, so she quietly leans him against the building wall to use his silent automatic pistol, shooting them both. Creinna yells to him to get up, Conner strains to find his footing, maneuvering through high terrain grass, nine guards are scattered at the water's edge. She lightly taps him moving her fingers in military form . "let's use our knives for the three standing in front of us. The other men are a mere distance apart. He nods, while both of them sneaked up and attacked cutting the guard's throats. One guard was still able to hear the commotion, Creinna and Conner made a break for it, jumping into the river bank. Six men rushed over firing into the water. Creinna and Conner managed to swim emerging, from the other side crawling out. Davien received a transmission call telling him what happened. He forwards back, "worthless shity helpers, I've ever seen, well forget them we have a fleet coming in our orbit, focus on that would ya!. "

CONNER SLOWED DOWN collapsing revealing he caught two stray bullets in his back. His voice began to rattle with a seizing sound. she pulls up his damped t-shirt to inspecting his wounds. Crienna closed her eyes with tears dripping down her face. Cradling Conner, he makes an ironic remark. "IF I'm going to go out, it might as well be like this, in a beautiful women's arms but don't tell my wife I said that." Creinna laughs while holding back tears, Conner adds a dying wish for Creinna to deliver, "tell my family I love them, and for my mom not to blame herself for this okay, (Creinna shakes her head).

"RACHEL LEAVE ME HERE save yourself, it's not safe out in the open. go ahead I'll be fine. Go, now!" Creinna gets up and walks backward saying goodbye. She reaches only midway towards the trees when a big loud bang goes off, Conner took his own life. She kept moving forward with an Air fleet just above her head arriving with several strike teams closing off their escape routes. Davien tells his Clients, "this is the day, you learn to hit and run. Once we set off the roof missiles against the air fleet, those who surround the building will give us some ammo support, if they're still alive. Then we could disappear underneath this floor bunker, which I installed a while back in case of an emergency like this, leading us out of a sewage pipeline. Now I know it's not ideal, but we want to survive right?. So, we're going to stay as long enough to help our men fight through opening patch holes of these windows. Just until we can get each of us out of

here safely." One shouts out in fear amongst them, " why can't we leave now, while there's still a chance? you've got guards outside, just like you mentioned." Davien tries to break it down for him. "if a big chunk of us decide to leave, all at once we risk getting caught. It's not so much, my men can do outside, in order to protect all of us inside here, therefore if we lend a hand. Then each section out of three, can leave one at a time, are you comprehending it now? Any more stupid questions?"

Felicia, Seth, and Daniel, along with Christopher sneaks up the southwest side quadrant. Radioing the other groups, Felicia commands to know their status. All three units, radio in saying they've reached their destinations. She gives her air fleet the okay to start firing. Davien's men turn on their 10 automatic machine guns toward the aircraft's. As his men began to attack incoming units from all sides. Davien orders the men inside to hold their position until they receive word from outside to shoot. Nerves pulse through the room hearing, guards outside yelling and screaming over the walkie-talkie intercom. Finally, 15 minutes in Davien got word. Davien picks up his gun, to the door window. Yelling "firer!", Creinna could hear rainfall of guns firing.

As she makes it to the airstrip to hop on Carmon's private helicopter. bullets blaze in a distant roar, while Davien tells the first group to leave.

Felicia calls to her air fleet commander. " Captain Norwin, a beacon movement reading of Conner, and Rachel has been detected outside the hotel premises on Christopher's watch notification. Showing non-civilian activity only Davien, and his crew members remain inside. It's no longer entitled as a retrieval rescue assignment. So, let's pull an audible, disarm those automatic guns on the roof and send a bomb inside dead, or alive he's leaving with us today." The fleet rapidly responds to her request: "Roger, Roger ringleader firing at will". Davien signals the third group to leave, when he sees a small missile deployed, coming in through the window. fast reflexes submerged over him as he jumps rushing underneath his bunker. A big erupting explosion, blew out shattering glass while smoke covered portions of surrounding areas. Davien assumed the tunnel pipelines would be strong enough to hold. But the structured building collapsed as nine men within the 3rd group got crushed, beneath large boulders. Davien and the first two groups made it out barely unscathed trying to escape, as the second fleet submerged, out from tall weeded bushes cutting them off.

CHRISTOPHER ASKED DAVIEN demandingly *"where are Rachel and Conner?"* Yelling, *"Where's my brother?"* Davien still appeared to be suffering from whiplash following the explosion. He answered honestly, *"they escaped before everything happened".* The officers then boarded Davien on a helicopter heading back to Seattle. Felicia replies to him *"we will find your brother".* He answered back, *"I don't believe his lying statistical mouth, not for one second".* One of the strike team officers pulls, Felicia to a side while Seth and Daniel console him. Giving her the disappointing news about Conner's body being found across a water bank, half a mile from where they are standing now. Felicia tells them *"not a word until we get back to their precinct, is that clear, not a word."* The agents responded, *"yes mam!"*

Chapter 6
A sad journey home

RIDING HOME CRIENNA'S mind was still wheeling on how to explain Conners's death to Carmon. Approaching her house through the gates she got an alert in her car surveillance feed which detected armed men vandalizing her home. She notices they are a part of the Triad, backing out slowly of her driveway, and turning around to call Christopher.

But no answer only his voicemail came through, she couldn't go to her job because that's the second place they will look. So she hides in her car inside a local park, with a gun laying nearby. As she closes her eyes to rest.

Felicia orders a unit to fly Davien to CIA headquarters, so she could debrief Christopher about his brother's condition. Chief Thomas was filled in first.

Felicia notify Christopher in the conference room as screams echoed throughout the halls, Daniel held him as he was falling onto his knees in pain. Seth bent down in front of him.

All three men stood in silence, as Chief Thomas stands next to the door. Seth and Daniel were sitting on opposite sides with Christopher while Felicia left for the agency. Christopher finally broke his silence saying, "can't lose my mother too, just can't." Chief Thomas responds "you won't," Seth says "yeah, no more losing anybody else." Daniel smiled agreeing, "I got your back bro." Christopher looked at his phone and realized he has 14 missed messages from Rachel, all three men hurried to meet her in the park.

Seth got out of the driver's side, from his truck running behind Daniel and Christopher approaching a similar identical car to Creinna's. Christopher knocked on her car door, as she gets out hugging him. Seth's thoughts were racing along with his heart in shock, realizing Rachel was none other than Creinna. Seth calls her name, while she lets go of Christopher abruptly. "OH, hell Na! Creinna your Rachel, you were his informant, this whole entire time." Creinna searches for words fumbling in a distraught voice. "Seth, wait I, I wanted to tell you."

Christopher looks at her, asking in confusion "Hold up, you two know each other, and why is he calling you Creinna?" Daniel catches Seth saying "not here bro, not in public we don't know who is watching us or, listening to us right now, come on. Hey! both of you, get in her car and follow us."

Daniel takes over driving. Seth hits the dashboard with his fist three times and leans back into the passager seat. Griping his hands over his mouth in horrifying disbelief, shedding tears. "Seth yells, dame it, why her, god why her? I thought she was perfect! You know, like I finally found somebody, instead, I found a liar and, a Cat burglar worse off than Lena." Daniel touched his friend's shoulder trying to give him encouraging words. "Seth no one is perfect, as a matter of fact. Conner and his mother aren't perfect, but Christopher still tried to save his family anyway. Tiffany lied about wearing those ugly mud facial masks, when we first started dating, making weird wheezing-like noises as she slept." (Seth gave Daniel a disappointed expression), "Is there a point to this? Cause I'm not really getting it ." Daniel tries giving him another point. " Seth no matter what happens in life, no one will ever be perfect, we weren't designed that way. I hope you can give her a chance to explain at least, and if it still doesn't sit well, with you then leave her alone. But at least remember Christopher made a mistake and now he is trying to turn his life around." Seth speaks in an odd state, "I hear you but I still need time to wrap my head around this shit."

Making it back to the precinct. Creinna parked her car. Jumping out of the driver's seat, and running to Seth, when he ferociously tells her, "don't touch me, I don't want to speak to you". Daniel leaps between them, as Seth heads inside the building. Daniel tries to claim her down, "Listen he needs time to calm himself." (Creinna explains to Daniel her alias name during business), "My alias name, is Rachal Bennett, I gave Seth my authentic name. Eventually, I was going to unveil the truth, with some prolonged dating. I never wanted this to tear us apart." Christopher stared at the situation when Daniel was trying to talk to her. "Stop! this isn't a good time to discuss this anyway Creinna. Our main priority now is to get you two in a safe house until this case completely blows over, because if it's true about the Triad. Then this fucked up scenario should be the least of your worries. I will convey your concerns to him. And see if you two can reach some kind of conclusion but for now, communication is off-limits." Christopher tells her 'be patient, give him some space."

SETH GOES ON THE ROOF to gain clarity, and Daniel followed him. "A horror movie just played out in my heart, and I was the main character, and of course, Creinna is casting as a diabolical villain. Can't debut a story without one, she's a class act pioneer. Daniel disrupts Seth, I'm not a therapist, in fact, I suck at it, but given the horror movie you've endured for 3 years, cause of Lena, your heroic heart deserves a happy ending. Even if it means hearing the horrifying villain out."

He shakes his head saying, "Na, na, man! my ears are slammed shut, for whatever lame-ass excuses, she's got going. Only Lies pouring like a waterfall." Daniel diverts to pleasant memories, "Well what about how she helped you come out of your shell? Look! we both know what she has done wasn't justifiable, by double agenting herself with Christopher and his family. But let's just say, for argument's sake. That she might get off with minor charges, and you two still can be together. Just keep the faith Seth, things have their own way, of working themselves out." Seth reiterated's "she broked me, Daniel just her face alone, is what did it. I don't know." Daniel remarks "even a broken heart can be fixed, like a damaged object in need of a repair, or a car that won't start needs a tune-up by a mechanic. Rather you admit it, or not. Creinna could still potentially be your doctor, it's just your decision, to expect the surgery." Seth tears up shifting his head downward. "What if it can't, what if it can't be repaired?". Daniel got in front of him putting his hands on his shoulders. "Love conquerors all man, Just look at me and Tiffeny we've been through hurdles of all kinds. Maybe not exactly like you and, Creinna but what couple hasn't, you're not going to be the first, and your dame! sure aren't going to be the last." Daniel walks downstairs, leaving Seth to marinate on what he'd said.

Coming back from the roof, Seth sneaks to Daniel standing on the back wall during a meeting, Chief Thomas was holding. talking softly, "you laid some deep profound poetic words on me, back there homie, I appreciated. After this meeting is over, I'll go rehash it with Creinna." Daniel smiles saying "don't mention it". Seth walks into a private room where Creinna was being held. As she turns in her chair setting down hand-cuffed at a table, astonished to see Seth sitting down across from her. He began to ask Creinna questions. "Frist off I'm going to need you to explain how this whole thing transpired." Creinna crouched her face feeling ashamed, but scrambled for words. "After graduating college, I needed funds to invest in my business. So having learned computer technician I decided to do favors on the side for friends, who I knew dealt with password problems to hacking databases. But it was only when, I established my jewelry business, less than 9 years after gaining over 3.7 million dollars, that's when I considered pulling the plug on my side hustle endeavors. But one of my employees introduced me to Carmon. She seemed like a sweet lady in desperate need of help. So, I completed three diamond heist jobs for her, and when I tried to end things, she threatened to leak sensitive confidential files about all of my clients including blackmailing me and my employees."

"IN ORDER FOR CARMON'S Silent, I had to become her lapdog, doing her bidding. Luckily during a heist, I was captured by Christopher who cut a deal with me to double agent to stop, his own mother from gunning for Davien, he promised me the Fed's could wipe my slate clean. If I partnered to help him and the Feds, detain his family members, I instantly accepted." Seth puzzled adding to her conclusion. "For one, you made a deal with the devil, you got caught with your hands in the cookie jar, being greedy and selfish wanting more. Two! let's not forget a royal mansion squeaky clean enough, to put any of our living accommodations here to shame, and a fridge stocked to feed countless people around the entire world plus armies. Four! pulling the wool over my eyes, and not being satisfied for what, you could have had, or what you, could have worked for." Unconsolable, Creinna sobbed pleading for, forgiveness. "Seth it was stupidity at its finest, but if you could find any ounce of compassion to remember our times together. Even now, I didn't pretend or fake it. Yes, I made a mistake but for you, for us. I forfeit riches, surrender eternity for a trophy of our love scored on my heart. Traveling back in time doesn't exist, but if it was real, erasing bad parts would be the first thing I'd do. keeping only you and I fully attached, burning inside my brain, I'm sorry Seth". He gets up gripping both hands to his waist.

Thinking of some way to help Creinna, pacing back and forth, "we have to hire a good lawyer because no matter how good your speech sounds right now, the jury is going to shove you under a bus. Burying you alive Creinna, and the Judges here are ruthless. They don't give a rat's penny about your poetry and how sweet it sounds. Oh! and before I forget, this counts as number five". Creinna tips her eyes upward to Seth " wait! you're still going to help me?" Seth bent his mouth in, releasing anxiety, " yes a friend reminded me that we're not perfect, but it's up to the person, to want to alter their lifestyle. Now Creinna if there's any chance you can make it out of this, by liquidating assets or even dang near getting a job working with the Feds for a plea deal, you take it, you hear me, For us! you accept it, otherwise, it's a no-go!" Creinna jumps up handcuffed to hug Seth, he pulls her back " I'm going to relay the same conversation to Christopher, don't admit to anything and to no one until I find a lawyer." (He walks out to call Felicia.)

Seth shares his plans to Felicia about putting Christopher and Cerinna permanently on, as criminal undercover agents. In order, to find the rest of the Triad members. And cutting more additional charges from their parole, Felicia tells him, "I'll see if I can talk to my Chief Director for coming back to the table, to readvise Christopher's contract along with Creinna's situation, whether or not we can retain them on our roster. But I'm not promising any guarantees it will work Seth. So let's not get ahead of ourselves okay." (Seth blows in relief responding back to her), "I understand thanks." He hangs up, filling in Daniel.

WHILE OFFICER, LIMMERMAN *lies to the prison guards about Seth telling him to relocate Christopher and Creinna to another part of the precinct crosstown. He began leading them down to the garage inside a black patrol van heading out. Seth storms into Creinna's holding room exited after talking to Daniel. Realizing she was gone,*

asking the guards where she was. They strangely gazed at Seth and told him about officer Limmerman. Seth comprehending now, he was a rogue Triad cop. He urgently runs back to Daniel, both men hopped in the truck pulling off behind them and tracking his GPS.

Daniel turns worried speaking to Seth," send a text to make sure the unit doesn't follow us too closely, " spooking this guy could wind up jeopardizing Christopher and Creinna's life. Seth sends a message to Chief Thomas to forward it to the S.w.a.t team, and Felicia.

Christopher begins to panic noticing it didn't appear to be a precinct building but a Farmhouse. Officer Limmerman pulls up while armed men, begin to circulate the van, sliding open the doors bringing them into a basement, and tieing them up securely along with Davien's Gardner, hitman, and her running mate Iyana James.

GEORGIA COMES DOWN as her guards stood aside making an opening aisle passage while holding guns, as Georgia speaks with delight. "Davien failed countless times trying killing you Christopher, and your precious informant, but there's no need to reminisce on the past, now is there? because in the next two days I'm going to become mayor again. Running Triad business shipments like clockwork as if nothing ever happened, Davien on the other hand, well I don't know, the Triad might end up killing him. He's been a stick up my spine for a while now, so good riddance. Come here babe, you did an excellent job getting them out of the pen unnoticed. Now go back before anyone figures out your missing okay." (Officer Limmerman kisses Georgia to head back.) Woowa! now that's what I call hired help people. Not lifting a finger messing up my manicures or Pedi. Stress can do more harm than good. You see these barrel cans behind me, its Concentrated gasoline strapped tight to C4, nothing but the best for my running mate, going out in style, with a bang. It looks like, 4th of July is coming early, for all of you special kids. Oops! It's getting late for my campaign

party tonight, you know shaking hands, kissing hideous fat babies the usual."

IYANA IS TERRIFIED and reluctant to speak, "my perception of you Georgia was never this to leave innocent bystanders to die. I've seen a brilliant woman who wanted to reshape our city and give opportunities to those who are less fortunate than us, to one day do, what we couldn't finish. Being mayor is not something you gain for greed but to restore order to people's faith in our government and legislature." Georgia laughs out loud with her men chiming in, "Lady preach to the choir if you want money? understand drugs are embedded in this so-called goodwill and harmonious society. wake up sweetie, what you dwell on is not real, okay, green makes the world go round, and since this dreadful lecture won't be hard amongst anyone else's ears. Which thank God for that! I will be busy taking center stage where my opinion. Will be the only thing that matters," Christopher scuffs in his seat channeling his hot-tempered face upon Georgia, she leaps back a little stunned at his failed efforts. " Wow look at this fine piece of a specimen, it's a dame shame you have to go to waste. But as you've witnessed, I'm seeing someone." Christopher lashed out, "6 feet under is where I'm going to put you, for my brother's life you sick twisted bitch!,." Georgia articulates back, this one has a nasty mouthpiece, oh well! it's only one way to solve it." She asked one of her men to toss her a piece of scotch tape to mound his mouth together. Creinna utters "even if you become mayor again, the internal affairs will eventually puzzle a trial back to you," Georgia gets aggravated flinging her finger and giving her men orders to duct tape the remaining. Georgia starts to demonstrate her plans once again from earlier. "Now! there is a fuze drawstring connected mid-way on the back wall, once the gasoline fills up the room, with all of you trapped inside here. then Kaboom! no more scum bags like you, pretty thought-out plan, right? If I do, say so myself. Everyone

catches my drift. Alright, awesome bye, bye crispy fritters, see you in the next life or not?" Two guards rushed to separately perform each task, one guard lit the fuse while the other punched holes in the gasoline Barrels.

A limousine appeared, to pick up Georgia and her crew, as they screamed and Mumbled, the unit ends up cutting officer Limmerman off fleeing back towards town, as Seth jumps out with his gun demanding answers and cuffing him. Officer Limmerman cracks a smile, "Liberation is served," Seth uncontrollably grabs his collar and shouts, "Where are they?" Meanwhile, Christopher and the others struggle to get freed. He detects a dull triangled pointed nail exposed out of the metal behind him on the bottom stairway so he scoots his chair further towards it, as gasoline gushingly flows leveling up to his knees. He knew dreadfully he had to get down, near the woodland piece inside the liquid. He then tips his chair over, lifting his face upward sawing both hands back and forth in a fast manner. Felicia stopped Seth and Daniel from interrogating officer Limmerman to show them a piggyback signal from her tech analyst, who somehow managed to track Christopher's last location from his skin barcode sealed on his left wrist when he was first recruited. Agent Tech Analysis Brody Morris informs, giving them the coordinates. "Based on Christopher's barcode scans, it's a pining location shown in the direction nearby a highway northeast of us, where only one Plantation farmhouse resides." Daniel riffled his fingers up saying "Let's go,".

STRONG FUMES FROM THE gasoline tires Christopher out, as the liquid solution, almost reaches half his face, he tries to quiver his head to stay conscious. But both of his hands slowly start to weigh down, as his head starts to tilt a little in the gasoline. Then suddenly to his surprise, he heard footsteps above the basement. As agent Felicia's voice echoed charging in, when Christopher quickly wiggled coming too,

mumbling hard as the others did. As the unit searched the plantation house. Felicia ducks inside near a kitchen pantry, but during her inspection, she unexpectedly hears whaling sounds coming from underneath the floor joist. Felicia yells to her team asking "is there a basement in here?". Agent Brody pulls up his map locator to get a visual of the Plantation floor plan and he responds "yes! it's behind a tiny cropped door near a staircase as we first entered". Rushing down she noticed all five of them tied up and soaked in gasoline, she quickly rushed to put out the fuze. While the other agents retrieve them up above surface grounds. Christopher fills in Felicia about Gegoria's plans to steal the election. Seth grabs and hugs Creinna, examining her entire body to make sure she was okay.

Georgia celebrates on stage giving a heartfelt warming speech to her supporters, holding a glass of champagne, she sees agents drifting down all aisles, between the crowd, and on both sides of the stage curtains barricading her in. Felicia walks on, towards her grabbing the mic and telling everyone to go home. She proceeds to put cuffs on Gegiora and hauling her off. As the agents made a square around her guards arresting them too.

CHAPTER 7 JUSTICE PREVAILS

CAPTURING CARMON THREE days later attempting to escape Napa valley airport in California, the head Director decided to continue Christopher and Creinna's contract, to round up other professional thieves compared in their line of abilities, cutting 10 out of 20 years sentencing. Only allowing them to permanently work off the remaining as criminal investigating agents. Wearing ankle-monitored

bracelets, letting them stay on Creinna's property being heavily guarded, and using them when there is a high-class mission involved. Christopher's mother's sentence was reduced by nine years from 30 years, leaving his youngest sister Olivia in the care of his brother's wife while attending boarding school in Europe. While Davien Besten will serve out his full judgment sentence of 80 years to life without parole. For use of gun possession, multiple counts of first-degree murders, stolen drugs, and diamond possession along with smuggling illegally in, and out of state county lines. Aggravated assault and battery, money laundering, kidnapping, sexual assault, human trafficking, and last but not least carjacking. Georgia is serving 75 years for portraying as a local official, kidnapping, drug smuggling, and murder of first degree as well. Rouge agents and officer Limmerman along with Davien's hit women assailant are receiving a maximum of 60 years for imprisonment.

CHIEF THOMAS HELD A meeting congratulating his officers, on a job well done "All the responsible criminal thus far has been accounted for even in Singapore, and especially here with Georgia Fields, the hit-women, and officer Limmerman, including any other rogue agents in the CIA. Good work to each, and every last one of you. More pay raises will come just not now, but let me stop being silly. Being a Chief growing up here has been a road of achievements. But it turned out to be more than just a bucket list, it became a privilege, a family. Raise your glass for the number one police department in this God-damn city!" (every cop poured in a cheerful grunt). Later, Mayor Iyana invites the entire police division to her winning camping party, but before attending Daniel and Seth decide's to see Davien one last time.

DAVIEN RECOGNIZES THAT Seth and Daniel came to poke fun before the Fed's hall him off to prison. He holds the bars pressing his face against the cell polls, staring while calling them out. "Well if it isn't Danielle and Sally". Daniel reacts back "it's Daniel and Seth," Davien wearing a smirk commenting "Whatever! looking like two Decked-out penguins going to join a circus, both of your mamas must have been coached strong by your midget dead-beat daddies, because you two came out of the birth canal deformed. Both of you need to crawl back up their wombs and bake some more, cause nothing about you two chimpanzees is finished cooking." Daniel gets upset trouting words back, "I see comedic Castrated Godfather is forming jokes this evening Bro, you see that?." Seth chimes in, "yeah! I see the Juvenile delinquent has jokes. Well, at least we aren't the ones going to prison, zipped up tight in a jumpsuit posing like an ill-sick constipated tangerine. Gonna be a while for a colonoscopy homie if any." "Daniel tag-teams back in with more insults: yeah but I doubt any doctors would want to check out his raggedy condescending butthole." Davien shouts adding," Yo I got family in different parts of area codes fool, so I won't be residing here long, and I also accept conjugal visits Sally so be sure to mention it, to your lady friend cause we have some unfinished business to attend to! tell her if she ever needs a stallion to break her spine, I'll do her a solid. I'll do my proper due diligence as a true man, because that little worm you trying to swing with, ain't going to hit on it correctly, but this joystick will. 100% guaranteed satisfaction, or, her money back. Except she wouldn't want to refund her purchase, because it would have been just that dame good Sally boy." Seth retaliates rudely, "a real woman needs a hero energizer, and I'm not talking about your dried-up low battery inflated rabbit ass. A zero, running on "E" all the time without a functional gas gauge," Daniel jumps in again.

"That's if he can even make it on top of her, you would have to lose a little bit of weight strumpet, so you won't have a massive heart attack before climaxing. Peeling over like a roach who just got sprayed

with a can filled with Raid poisoning, Oh wait Carmon was trying to pull the same exact scheme out on you right, Hum? if only she would have succeeded. Got people scared running in the streets, labeling you a dame ghost. Well, ghost my ass, bet you can't squeeze your tubby behind, through those steel-plated beamed bars. Now can you?" Davien frowns returning warning threats, "Well stranger miracles have happened if you believe enough. So, don't count me out just yet. But anyway don't worry empty jokes won't faze my kids. One call, soon as I get a chance to speak with my lawyer, remember I still have rights. You will be choking on your words son, believe it. Then I'll skin your bones raw. Once I get loose partner, keep talking yall shit."

Daniel replies "Oh you lucky dog you, we all know a man of your Grandpa crippled stature, would have full-grown Gremlins running out of wedlock, we have plenty of room". Seth grins agreeing with Daniel "yeah as a matter of fact six hundred and seventy-two to be exact, it will be a whole family affair all locked up here together eating slop and rotting in their own filth. While the rodents tease yall sorry crackheads at night". Both men laughed slapping their knees, high-fiving each other. As Davien rams his fist against the bars <u>Fussing Profusely</u>. Seth and Daniel start to leave out the chamber cell doors. Davien threatens them with one last-minute rant. " Hey, those were some bold ass words you been spewing outside these bars, why don't you come back here and unlock them and say it to my mother f****** face, cause you will never be rid of this demon, never, Never!." The guards close the doors behind them as they head out to celebrate Mayor Iyana's campaign win. After the party Seth knocks on Criennas door, she comes up opening it, wearing down her sandy long brown hair, with a sexy white tank top, and light tropical booty low-cut spandex shorts on. Paired with pink slippers, and a house arrest monitor strapped to her right ankle. He leans his shoulders to the left side door, raising his right hand and holding a brown paper bag filled with take-out Chinese, saying. "I figured you might need a sleepover nightcap". She grabs his *black tie pulling him inside towards her for a kiss while shutting the door behind them using her left foot.*

Once inside Creinna glares him up and down, telling him to wait in the living room while she puts her Chinese food in the fridge. When returned, she grabbed Seth guiding him upstairs to her room. He stood excitedly as Creinna cuts on a bedroom record set to replay. As she kissed Seth's neck and lips. Loosening up his belt to unfasten his pants. Seth quickly grabs her in a hunger fixation throwing Creinna on the bed rubbing his fingers underneath her ting top bra and exposing her upper left nipple breast slowly kissing it passionately. Creinna combs her hands through his hair, while he continues to trace down his tongue gradually smooching her stomach area. Sliding her laced under ware free, and pulling off the rest of his clothing. Creinna also disposes away with her bra, he comfortably takes his time holding her right wrist, using his left hand to penetrate below with two fingers extracting partly in and out of her emotionally for twelve minutes. Crienna's fist clutches together in ecstasy. As he watches on in satisfaction, Seth suddenly stops and pulls her up apond his thighs. To take over from there kissing in a slightly enticing manner placing his hands and fingers spread out, tightly holding Creinna's butt. Reeling in a pounding upward fast cropped position, for no longer than ten minutes, rolling her face down with her neck and shoulders bent a little to her left on the pillow. She braces as he crossed both of her arms laying on her backside. While he thrust intensely from the back for a few moments. Now shifting her over with both their eyes locked on each other. She places one of his fingers inside her mouth lusting for more, he then gallantly moves inward and out between her legs. Creinna pours out a yarning cry as her legs quiver. Seth feeds his hands into hers filled with contentment throughout the nightly evening.

ONE YEAR LATER HE SITS calmly in an airport lobby waiting for Crienna's arrival from her mission overseas. Peering out of the crowd wearing a full-length black-sleeved agent suit with Christopher behind her, Crienna runs leaping in Seth's arms and kissing him. Christopher begins to roll his eyes saying "Hey are you two going to carry this home instead of showing and telling it to the whole nation because I also have a girlfriend to get home to". Seth takes her duffle bag as they walk out towards his truck, putting their luggage inside, but handing over his keys, winking at Christopher asking him to follow behind. Creinna felt awkward with Seth's strange attitude and behavior. "What devilment plots are you up to now?" Seth adds more to her curiosity. "Nothing, he's just coming to join us for a bite to eat, before heading home. While we're taking a Taxi cab instead." Creinna is still not convinced. "He lives with us, so why are we driving in two separate vehicles, it doesn't make sense?" she knew something fishy was wrong. "Okay, Mr. Ross I'll go along with your crazy charade for now". Seth gives Christopher a thumbs up. The Taxi cab stopped in front of Boenolee's, where their first date took place. Both Seth and Creinna got out walking in, as the whole unit and her family yelled "surprise". Seth immediately got down on one knee. "who would have guessed Boenolee's? A designated spot could start a new chapter in our lives, after 4 years of worrying there wouldn't be someone special to light up my soul from Lena's damage and bring fulfillment to my heart. Then I met you Creinna, I kneel down, not as a man, but as a person who wants to spend the rest of his life with you. Please, will you do me the honor of becoming my wife?" Creinna smiled with tears glossing her eyes. "Yes, babe I'll marry you".

He pretends to slide the ring on her finger building up more suspense. "I don't think this ring should be slipped on quite just yet, because there's one last thing you would have to do first. There is a white dress in the back of the lady's room waiting for you to put it on, so you can come back here to make us legally official." Crienna's mom Abbeygale gently takes her daughter's right hand to guide her to the back to get dressed. Her dad Lionel walks her down the aisle, towards Seth, standing behind him, is his brother Aden titled best man. Daniel and Christopher lobbied as his groom men, they exchanged vows as his ordained priest announced them, man and wife.

AFTERWARD, SETH PULLED Creinna onto the dance floor. Tiffany tugged on Daniels's bow tie luring him to the floor, when Christopher also grabs Felicia twirling her with a dip. While everyone else soon followed suit on the celebration and ringed little tiny silvered bells. Chanting "kiss, kiss, kiss," He soothes his hands across her cheeks romantically kissing ending old past memories with a new future.

The End